MW00901666

THE ADVENTURES OF DYNAMO THE DOBERMAN:
A TAIL-WAGGING TALE

BELONGS TO

....

Copyright © 2023 Emma afia. All rights reserved. No part of this publication may be reproduced, stored in a retrieval system, or transmitted in any form or by any means, electronic, mechanical, photocopying, recording, or otherwise, without the prior written permission of the copyright owner. This book is sold subject to the condition that it shall not be resold, lent, hired out or otherwise circulated without the publisher's prior consent in any form of binding or cover other than that in which it is published and without a similar condition including this condition being imposed on the subsequent purchaser.

This is a work of fiction. Names, characters, businesses, organizations, places, events, and incidents either are the product of the author's imagination or are used fictitiously. Any resemblance to actual persons, living or dead, events, or locales is entirely coincidental.

The following trademarked terms are mentioned in this book: Emma Afia. The use of these trademarks does not indicate an endorsement of this work by the trademark owners. The trademarks are used in a purely descriptive sense and all trademark rights remain with the trademark owner.

Cover design by el Emma afia.

This book was typeset in Emma afia.

First edition, 2023.

Published by Emma Afia.

Chapter 1: A Lively Arrival

- Introduction to Dynamo, the energetic and playful Doberman puppy.
- Dynamo's adoption by a kind family and his arrival at his new home.
- Dynamo's initial adventures in exploring his surroundings, meeting the family members, and bonding with them.

Chapter 2: Dynamo's Playful Pals

- Dynamo's encounter with other animals in his neighborhood, such as a mischievous squirrel, a friendly cat, and a wise old owl.
- Dynamo's playful interactions and forming unlikely friendships with these animals.
- Learning lessons about respecting boundaries, communication, and the importance of empathy.

Chapter 3: Dynamo Unleashed

- Dynamo's first adventure beyond his neighborhood as he accidentally slips out of the gate.
- Dynamo's exploration of the nearby park, encountering new sights, sounds, and smells.
- A thrilling chase with some mischievous raccoons and Dynamo's triumphant return home.

Chapter 4: The Mystery of the Missing Bone

- Dynamo's quest to solve the mystery of his missing bone, which he buried in the backyard.
- Seeking clues, interviewing other pets in the neighborhood, and unraveling the truth.
- A surprising twist and the discovery of an unexpected culprit, teaching Dynamo the importance of forgiveness and problem-solving.

Chapter 5: Dynamo's Heroic Rescue

- Dynamo's bravery and quick thinking when he stumbles upon a trapped animal in a dangerous situation.
- The exciting rescue mission, involving teamwork and overcoming obstacles.
- Dynamo's recognition as a hero and the celebration of his courage and compassion.

Chapter 1

A Lively Arrival

Dynamo, the lively and adventurous Doberman puppy, couldn't contain his excitement as he arrived at his new home. With a wagging tail and a twinkle in his eyes, he bounded out of the car, ready to explore his new surroundings.

As Dynamo stepped foot into the house, he was greeted by a loving family who instantly fell in love with his playful nature. The children giggled as Dynamo showered them with wet puppy kisses, and his tail wagged furiously with joy.

Eager to explore, Dynamo began his adventure by investigating every nook and cranny of his new home. He poked his nose into every corner, sniffing the scents of his new family and wagging his tail in approval.

The family showed Dynamo his cozy dog bed and filled his bowl with delicious puppy food. Dynamo devoured his meal with gusto, wagging his tail with each bite. His family watched him with delight, knowing they had found the perfect companion.

After a satisfying meal, Dynamo was taken outside to a spacious backyard. His eyes widened with excitement as he saw a world of possibilities before him. He sprinted across the grass, his paws barely touching the ground, chasing his own tail in circles of pure joy.

As Dynamo's playful energy filled the air, the family laughed and clapped, encouraging his antics. They knew they had made the right choice by bringing Dynamo into their lives.

Exhausted from his adventures, Dynamo curled up in his dog bed, feeling safe and loved in his new home. With a contented sigh, he drifted off to sleep, dreaming of the many exciting adventures that awaited him.

Little did Dynamo know that his lively arrival was just the beginning of a remarkable journey filled with friendship, bravery, and unforgettable escapades.

Chapter 2

Dynamo's Playful Pals

The sun rose on another beautiful day, and Dynamo's tail wagged with anticipation. Eager to explore beyond the confines of his yard, Dynamo set off on a quest to make new friends in the neighborhood.

His first encounter was with a mischievous squirrel named Nutmeg. Dynamo's curious nose led him to a tree where Nutmeg was gathering acorns. Dynamo's ears perked up, and he barked playfully, inviting Nutmeg to join in the fun. Nutmeg, intrigued by Dynamo's enthusiasm, hopped down from the tree and began a game of chase. They raced around the yard, leaping over bushes and dodging trees. Dynamo had never felt such excitement before!

As Dynamo continued his adventures, he stumbled upon a graceful cat named Whiskers. Dynamo approached Whiskers cautiously, sniffing the air to gauge their potential friendship. To Dynamo's delight, Whiskers responded with a gentle purr and a swish of her tail. They spent hours together, pouncing on imaginary prey and sharing stories about their favorite hiding spots. Dynamo realized that cats could be friends too, and he cherished their newfound companionship.

One moonlit night, Dynamo spotted a wise old owl perched on a branch, observing the world below. Dynamo approached cautiously, his eyes wide with wonder. The owl, named Hoot, spoke in a calm and soothing voice. Hoot shared wisdom about the secrets of the night, teaching Dynamo to appreciate the beauty in darkness and the importance of listening. Dynamo realized that there was much to learn from creatures different from himself.

As Dynamo's friendships grew, he learned valuable lessons about respecting boundaries. He understood that squirrels needed trees to climb, cats needed quiet moments, and owls needed the night sky to spread their wings. Dynamo discovered that true friends understand and respect each other's needs, even if they can't always play together.

With each playful encounter, Dynamo's heart expanded with love and understanding. He discovered that friendship knows no boundaries and that different species can create a tapestry of companionship. Dynamo's playful pals taught him the power of empathy, communication, and the joy that comes from sharing laughter and adventures.

Little did Dynamo know, his playful pals were just the beginning of a lifelong bond and a series of extraordinary escapades that awaited him. With newfound wisdom and an open heart, Dynamo looked forward to the many adventures that lay ahead, grateful for the friends who had enriched his life.

Chapter 3

Dynamo Unleashed

One sunny morning, as Dynamo's family opened the gate to let him out for his usual romp in the backyard, an unexpected gust of wind blew the gate wide open. Before anyone could react, Dynamo darted out, his paws barely touching the ground. He had been unleashed into the world beyond his neighborhood. With a mix of excitement and trepidation, Dynamo found himself exploring a vast, unfamiliar park. The scents of nature surrounded him as he ventured deeper into the unknown. Butterflies fluttered by, teasing Dynamo to chase them, but he had other things on his mind.

As Dynamo trotted along a winding path, he stumbled upon a group of ducks waddling by a shimmering pond. Dynamo's eyes sparkled with curiosity. He cautiously approached the ducks, hoping to make some feathered friends. The ducks quacked and waddled away, but Dynamo persisted. He barked gently, trying to show them he meant no harm. Eventually, one friendly duck named Quackers waddled back towards Dynamo, and they exchanged a wag and a quack. Dynamo had made a friend from a different world!

The park was filled with new scents and sounds that captivated Dynamo's senses. He encountered squirrels scurrying up trees, their fluffy tails flicking mischievously. Dynamo gave chase, his excitement growing with every leap and bound. Though he never quite caught up to the agile squirrels, their game of chase brought endless laughter and joy.

As Dynamo ventured deeper into the park, he discovered a hidden grove where rabbits hopped and nibbled on the grass. Dynamo approached them with a friendly wag, hoping to join in their playful antics. The rabbits hopped away at first, but Dynamo's gentle persistence won them over. They soon hopped around him in a game of follow-the-leader, and Dynamo reveled in their fluffy companionship.

But amidst all the fun, Dynamo realized he had wandered far from home. Panic set in as he tried to retrace his steps, but the park seemed unfamiliar and vast. He felt a pang of worry, fearing he would never find his way back to his beloved family.

Just as hope began to fade, a kind-hearted jogger noticed Dynamo's distress. The jogger recognized the familiar look of a lost pup and approached with a warm smile. Dynamo's tail wagged with relief as the jogger scanned Dynamo's collar and called his family. Dynamo's family arrived shortly, their faces filled with relief and gratitude.

Dynamo's adventure in the park had taught him both the exhilaration of exploration and the importance of staying close to home. As he was safely escorted back to his family, Dynamo felt a renewed sense of gratitude for the love and security they provided.

From that day forward, Dynamo would always cherish the freedom of the park, but he would never forget the warm embrace of his home. The experience had instilled in him a newfound appreciation for the safety and love that his family offered, and he vowed to never wander too far again.

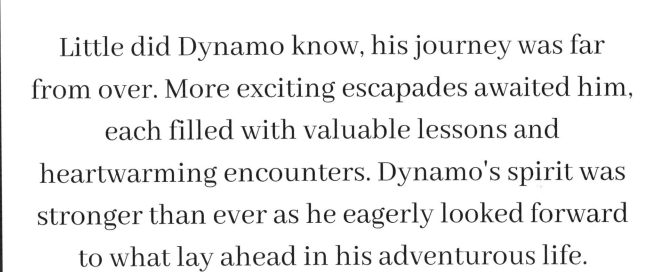

Little did Dynamo know, his journey was far from over. More exciting escapades awaited him, each filled with valuable lessons and heartwarming encounters. Dynamo's spirit was stronger than ever as he eagerly looked forward to what lay ahead in his adventurous life.

Chapter 4

The Mystery of the Missing Bone

It was a sunny day, and Dynamo decided it was the perfect time to bury his favorite bone in the backyard. With careful paws, he dug a hole and gently placed his prized possession inside. Dynamo was certain that his bone would be safe in its secret hiding spot.

The next day, Dynamo bounded into the backyard, eager to retrieve his bone and enjoy a satisfying chew. But to his surprise, the spot where he had buried it was empty. His bone had disappeared!

Confused and determined, Dynamo sniffed around, trying to uncover any clues. His nose led him to his mischievous feline friend, Whiskers, who was lazily sunning herself on the porch. Dynamo wagged his tail and asked if she had seen anything suspicious. Whiskers blinked lazily and denied any knowledge of the missing bone.

Undeterred, Dynamo continued his investigation. He approached his wise old friend, Hoot the owl, perched high in a tree. Dynamo described the disappearance of his bone, hoping Hoot would provide some insight. Hoot hooted thoughtfully and advised Dynamo to observe his surroundings more closely, as sometimes answers could be found where they were least expected.

Following Hoot's advice, Dynamo ventured into the neighborhood, questioning the local pets about his missing bone. Nutmeg the squirrel, who always seemed to be up to some mischief, claimed innocence and pointed Dynamo in a different direction. Dynamo was determined to solve the mystery and pressed on.

His search eventually led him to a secluded corner of the backyard where a small hole had been dug. Dynamo's ears perked up, and his heart raced with excitement. He sniffed the hole and discovered a faint scent of his bone. Someone had indeed taken it!

Suddenly, Dynamo noticed a familiar raccoon lurking nearby. It was Bandit, known for his sneaky antics and love for shiny objects. Dynamo growled, confronting Bandit about his missing bone. Bandit, caught off guard, confessed with a mischievous grin. He had been drawn to the glimmer of Dynamo's bone and couldn't resist the temptation. Dynamo's anger melted into understanding as Bandit explained that he was fascinated by shiny objects but hadn't meant any harm. Dynamo, realizing the value of forgiveness, decided to give Bandit a chance to make amends.

Together, Dynamo and Bandit devised a plan. Dynamo would share his toys and treasures with Bandit, satisfying his desire for shiny objects. In return, Bandit promised to never take Dynamo's bone again and to return any other stolen items to their rightful owners.

With their pact sealed, Dynamo's bone was returned to its rightful place in the backyard. Dynamo felt a sense of satisfaction and relief, knowing that he had not only solved the mystery but also found a way to turn a potential adversary into a friend.

From that day forward, Dynamo and Bandit became unlikely allies, sharing adventures and mischief, while also learning important lessons about forgiveness, trust, and the power of second chances.

The mystery of the missing bone had not only brought Dynamo's bone back but also taught him the value of understanding and compassion. Dynamo's heart swelled with gratitude for the friends he had made and the valuable life lessons he had learned along the way. Little did Dynamo know, more exciting escapades awaited him, each one filled with surprises and opportunities to grow.

Chapter 5

Dynamo's Heroic Rescue

On a cloudy afternoon, Dynamo set out for a walk with his family in a nearby forest. The air was crisp, and the scent of adventure filled Dynamo's nostrils. Little did he know that this would be the day he would embark on his most daring and heroic mission yet.

As Dynamo trotted along the forest trail, he noticed a distressed chirping sound coming from a dense thicket. His ears perked up, and his instinct to protect kicked in. Dynamo dashed toward the source of the sound and discovered a small bird tangled in a web spun by a crafty spider.

Without hesitation, Dynamo leaped into action. He carefully and gently gnawed away at the sticky strands, setting the frightened bird free. As the bird fluttered its wings and took flight, Dynamo felt a rush of satisfaction. He had saved a life!

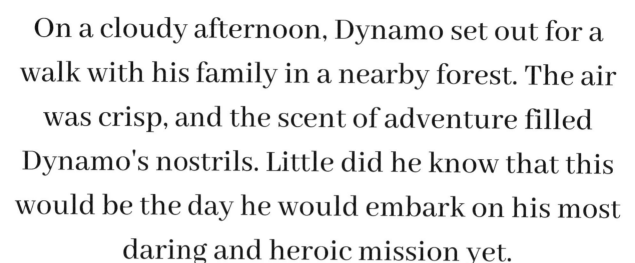

Word of Dynamo's heroic rescue spread through the forest, reaching the ears of a wise old turtle named Sheldon. Curious about the courageous pup, Sheldon approached Dynamo with a smile. He commended Dynamo for his bravery and explained that true heroes come in all shapes and sizes.

In awe of Sheldon's wisdom, Dynamo listened attentively as the turtle shared stories of other remarkable animal heroes. From dolphins rescuing stranded swimmers to elephants protecting their young from danger, Dynamo realized that acts of bravery were not limited to humans alone. Animals too had the power to make a difference.

Emboldened by his newfound knowledge, Dynamo decided to become a guardian of the forest, using his keen senses and boundless energy to protect and help those in need. He pledged to be a hero not just to his family but also to all the creatures who called the forest their home.

Dynamo's heroic reputation grew, and animals far and wide sought his help. He rescued a stranded frog from a treacherous pond, guided lost baby hedgehogs back to their nest, and even warned a family of deer about an approaching storm. Dynamo's acts of bravery and kindness inspired others to be courageous and compassionate.

With each successful rescue, Dynamo's confidence grew. He realized that being a hero was not about seeking recognition but about making a positive impact on the lives of others. The forest creatures admired Dynamo's selflessness and looked up to him as a true role model.

As the sun set, Dynamo returned to his family, his heart full of pride and joy. He shared his adventures with them, regaling them with tales of his heroic deeds. His family listened in awe, grateful to have such an extraordinary pup as part of their lives.

From that day forward, Dynamo embraced his role as the forest's guardian and continued to selflessly help those in need. His bravery, compassion, and unwavering spirit made him a beloved and respected figure among both animals and humans alike.

And so, Dynamo's tale of heroism serves as a reminder that anyone, no matter their size or species, can make a difference in the world. With a wag of his tail and a sparkle in his eyes, Dynamo's adventures continued, inspiring others to find the hero within themselves.

The End

Copyright © 2023 Emma afia. All rights reserved. No part of this publication may be reproduced, stored in a retrieval system, or transmitted in any form or by any means, electronic, mechanical, photocopying, recording, or otherwise, without the prior written permission of the copyright owner. This book is sold subject to the condition that it shall not be resold, lent, hired out or otherwise circulated without the publisher's prior consent in any form of binding or cover other than that in which it is published and without a similar condition including this condition being imposed on the subsequent purchaser.

This is a work of fiction. Names, characters, businesses, organizations, places, events, and incidents either are the product of the author's imagination or are used fictitiously. Any resemblance to actual persons, living or dead, events, or locales is entirely coincidental.

The following trademarked terms are mentioned in this book: Mohamed El Afia. The use of these trademarks does not indicate an endorsement of this work by the trademark owners. The trademarks are used in a purely descriptive sense and all trademark rights remain with the trademark owner.

Cover design by el Emma afia.

This book was typeset in Emma afia.

First edition, 2023.

Published by Emma Afia.

Made in the USA
Monee, IL
06 March 2024

54542481R00017